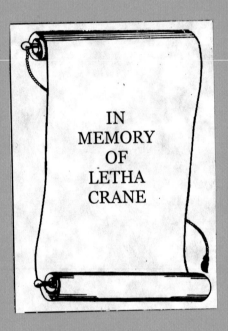

IN
MEMORY
OF
LETHA
CRANE

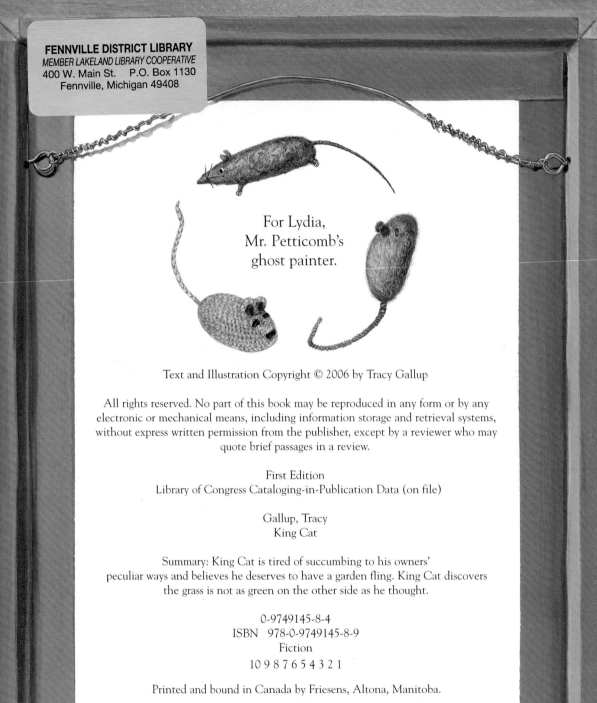

For Lydia,
Mr. Petticomb's
ghost painter.

Text and Illustration Copyright © 2006 by Tracy Gallup

First Edition
Library of Congress Cataloging-in-Publication Data (on file)

Gallup, Tracy
King Cat

Summary: King Cat is tired of succumbing to his owners'
peculiar ways and believes he deserves to have a garden fling. King Cat discovers
the grass is not as green on the other side as he thought.

0-9749145-8-4
ISBN   978-0-9749145-8-9
Fiction
10 9 8 7 6 5 4 3 2 1

Printed and bound in Canada by Friesens, Altona, Manitoba.

A Mackinac Island Press, Inc. publication, Traverse City, Michigan
www.mackinacislandpress.com

King Cat

Written & Illustrated by Tracy Gallup

Mrs. Petticomb walks in the garden
with flowers in her hat.

Mr. Petticomb goes one better...

...he wears me, the cat.

But wait just a moment, I am a beast,
not a common piece of clothing.
Another cat might be watching me,
snickering and loathing—

a cat who willingly spends his days,
indulging his owners' peculiar ways.

Owners! **Ha!** Who owns whom?
I rule garden and living room.

For I am King Cat,
sharp toothed growler, stealthy prowler,

and certainly not a living fur collar!

Adventure awaits!

This noble king deserves
to have a garden fling.

Dragonfly and bumblebee,
I am your ruling majesty.

Over birds and mice I reign.
This is my kingdom, my domain!

Who dare to sniff the regal rose?

I'd defend my turf, but there's rain on my nose.

I've been gone long enough
to be sorely missed,
and my velvet nose
prefers to be kissed.
Maybe they're worried.
I'd better go home...

...to Mr. and Mrs. Petticomb.

Royal cats don't like to get wet.

I am **King Cat!**

Don't ever forget—

to fill my bowl with salmon chow,
and listen when I say meow.

Will someone toss
my catnip mouse?

And stoke the fire!
It's cold in this house.
To walk upon my tender paws
insults my kingly pride,
So put me on your shoulders, please,

King Cat prefers to ride!

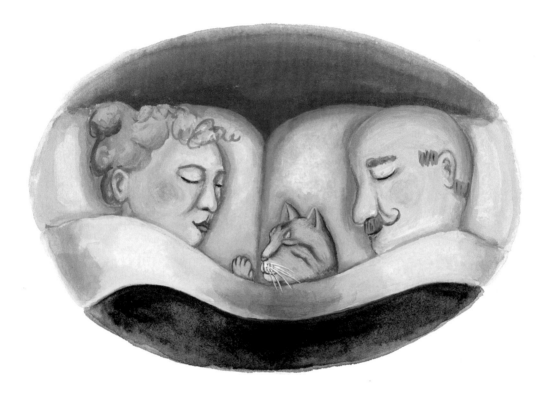